Because
he might
crack up.

Why couldn't Little Tommy Tucker eat his supper?

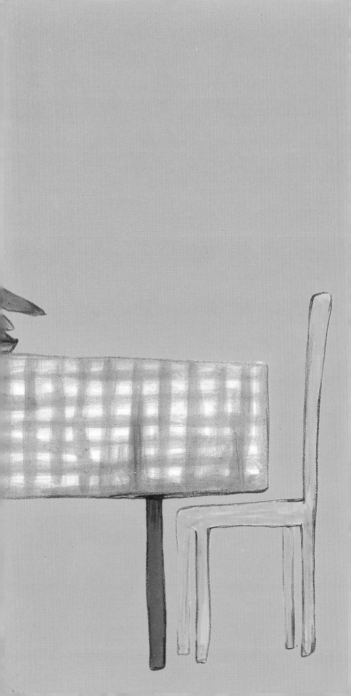

Because the dish ran
away with the spoon.

What instrument does Old Mother Hubbard's dog like to play?

The trombone.

Who waddled his men
up to the top of the hill
and down again?

The Grand Old
Duck of York.

What did the cow with the crumpled horn do when the house that Jack built was finished?

He "moo"ved in.

Where did the Three Little
Kittens find their lost mittens?

In their mother's
"purr"se.

What does Mother Goose do
when she's in a traffic jam?

She honks
her goose.

What woke Little Boy Blue
from his nap under
the haystack?

Little Bo's Peep

How does the Queen of Hearts keep her castle warm?

With Old
King's coa

What were the Butcher, the Baker, and the Candlestick Maker members of?

The rub-a-dub club.

Who did Jill call when Jack fell
down the hill?